Gunner's Boy

For David and Roberta

Gunner's Boy

Ann Turnbull

A & C Black • London

TUDOR FLASHBACKS
Boy King • David Belbin
Robbers on the Road • Melvin Burgess
The Eyes of Doctor Dee • Maggie Pearson
Gunner's Boy • Ann Turnbull

also available:
WORLD WAR II FLASHBACKS
The Right Moment • David Belbin
Final Victory • Herbie Brennan
Blitz Boys • Linda Newbery
Blood and Ice • Neil Tonge

VICTORIAN FLASHBACKS
Soldier's Son • Garry Kilworth
A Slip in Time • Maggie Pearson
Out of the Shadow • Margaret Nash
The Voyage of the Silver Bream • Theresa Tomlinson

First paperback edition 2003
First published in hardback 2002
by A & C Black Publishers Ltd
37 Soho Square, London, W1D 3QZ
www.acblack.com

ISBN 0-7136-6198-4

A CIP catalogue record for this book is available
from the British Library.

A & C Black uses paper produced with elemental, chlorine-free
pulp, harvested from managed sustainable forests.

Printed and bound in Great Britain by
Creative Print & Design (Wales), Ebbw Vale

Contents

Author's Note

In 1588 Spain was a Catholic country, but England, under Elizabeth I, was Protestant. Religion meant much more to people then than it does now, and Philip II of Spain believed that it was God's will that he should invade England and bring it back to the Catholic faith. Elizabeth also provoked Philip by sending her privateers to raid the Spanish colonies and steal treasure from Spanish galleons. Although the two countries were not at war, there were frequent outbreaks of hostilities at sea.

Boys as young as John served aboard both the Spanish and English ships. Some may have volunteered, but others would have been taken by a press-gang. These gangs were employed to seize men off the streets and force them to serve at sea.

The defeat of the Spanish Armada was celebrated as a great victory, but for the English Navy the Armada was a formidable enemy and victory was far from certain until, in the end, the weather came to England's aid.

The *Fortune* and the *Pearl* and their crews are

fictitious, but all the other ships in this story really existed, and the battles that John took part in are based on fact.

PLACES TO VISIT

THE *GOLDEN HINDE* at Southwark, London. A replica of the ship in which Drake sailed around the world. Although smaller than the galleons that defeated the Armada, it gives a good impression of conditions on board.

FIREPOWER at the Royal Arsenal, Woolwich, London. An exciting new museum of artillery through the ages, where you can see cannons like those used in 1588.

THE *MARY ROSE*, Henry VIII's flagship galleon, at Portsmouth; and the ROYAL NAVAL MUSEUM.

THE PLYMOUTH DOME. An interactive visitor centre that brings Plymouth's past to life.

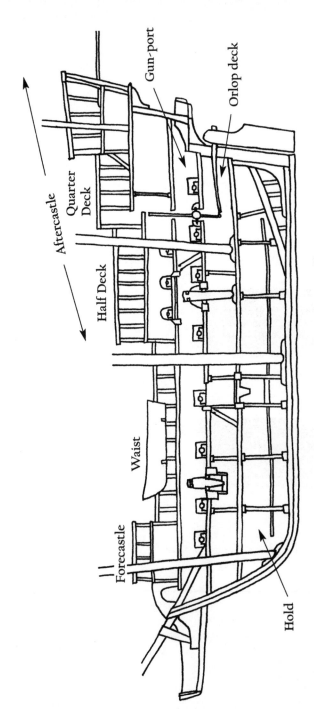

Cross-section of a sixteenth-century galleon

1 ❖ Wednesday 27th July 1588

John pushed through waist-high bracken and came out on the highway. He let the heavy bag slide from his shoulder, sinking down beside it.

He'd walked ten miles or more since leaving home at dawn. His whole body ached. His breeches and shoes were mud-spattered, his hands cut by brambles. And yet he felt happy. He was on his way to Plymouth to join the Royal Navy.

'You're too young!' his mother had protested.

But they both knew he wasn't. England and Spain were enemies. The Spanish Armada was coming: the beacons were manned and ready to fire as soon as it was sighted, and the fleet was taking on boys as young as twelve.

John's mother had packed his seaman's bag: a big drawstring bag full of bedding and spare clothes. She'd given him food for the journey and beer in a leather flask. She and his sister had come to the top of the cliff path to see him off. John had felt sorry to be leaving them, and yet nervous and eager to be going away.

He had hoped for a lift on the main road, and now he saw his chance: a cart, laden with sacks.

He stood up.

The carter reined in his horse. 'I can take you to Plymouth.'

'Thanks.'

John hefted his bag into the wagon and climbed up next to the carter.

'Come far?' the man asked.

'From Hope Cove. I'm going to enlist.'

'Seaman's son, are you?'

'Aye. My father was master's mate on a merchant ship. The *Pearl*, of Salcombe.'

'The *Pearl*? Wasn't that the ship—?'

'Yes. Last year. She was captured by the Spanish off the Netherlands. My father died in the fighting.'

And I'll have revenge, John promised himself. I'll join up and fight the Armada and avenge my father's death.

The wagon was slow, the road full of ruts and puddles, but they began to see more carts and people on horseback as they approached the town. They drove into the narrow, crowded streets and the cartwheels bumped over cobbles. John smelt the sea, and heard gulls crying.

The carter stopped outside an inn.

John thanked him, and sprang down. He hoisted his bag on to his shoulder and at once became part of the crowd. There were sailors, gentlefolk, shipwrights, gangs of pressed men, carts laden with barrels. He didn't need to ask the way to the harbour. Everyone seemed to be moving in that direction, and John was carried along by the tide of people. He turned a corner, and the seafront opened out before him.

And there, in the harbour, was the English fleet: a hundred ships or more – galleons, transports and supply ships. The galleons were painted in bright chequered patterns, blue and white, black and white, and one – he recognised Sir Francis Drake's ship, the *Revenge* – in green and white. Nearby was the *Triumph*, and Lord Howard's flagship, the *Ark Royal*.

John gazed at them all. So many famous ships – and he was about to join their company. He wanted to jump for joy.

But how was he to enlist? And on which ship?

He saw a blue and white painted galleon, the *Fortune*, smaller than the *Revenge* but with a powerful array of guns. Seamen carrying bags like his were going aboard. John stepped on to the gangplank and followed them.

A clerk sat at a table, taking names.

John felt a fluttering in his stomach. Would they take him on?

But the clerk merely glanced up and asked, 'Name?'

'John Amery, sir.'

'Age?'

'Thirteen, come September.'

The quill scratched on paper. 'Good. Your pay will be six shillings a month. Go below, and ask for Mr Gains.'

It was done. He was part of the crew on one of the Queen's ships. He felt the boards rocking beneath him and knew he would not stand on dry land again till the war was over.

'Out of the way, boy! Jump to it!'

A seaman was rolling a barrel across the deck, and more barrels were being hoisted up from a supply boat. John darted down the ladder to the gun deck.

He noticed the smell as he went down: a mixture of gunpowder, tar, sweat and bilge water. Even the open gun ports couldn't dispel it, though they gave some light.

The deck was low. John hit his head and had to remember to stoop as he walked through. There was noise – shouted orders, the clash of metal. Gunners, pikemen and musketeers were all moving about hunched over. Everyone seemed busy and self assured. John's confidence began to waver. As he stood uncertainly a man carrying a sack on his shoulders stopped beside him: a burly, sandy-haired man.

'You look lost, boy,' he said. 'Don't let Mr Gains catch you idle.'

'I must report to Mr Gains, sir.' John felt a tremor of anxiety.

The man indicated with a nod of his head, 'That's him over there – in the blue jacket. The boatswain.'

Mr Gains was a short, hard-faced man with a cold eye. His glance flicked over John. 'I've no time for you now. Where's Kerslake? KERSLAKE!'

A youth of about sixteen appeared. 'Sir?'

'Take Amery in hand. Show him what's to do. We could sail any day and I want no slackers.'

He turned away.

Kerslake looked down on John from his superior height. 'So they're bringing babes in now?'

'I'm near thirteen … sir,' said John.

Kerslake's lip curled. 'You don't have to call me "sir". Have you been to sea before, Mr Near-thirteen?'

'Once, s—' John checked himself. It was difficult not to say 'sir'; the youth was so big and his manner was so overbearing. 'Once. To Flanders.' John remembered that trip with longing. He'd thought it was the beginning of his working life with his father.

Kerslake ducked under the beams towards a ladder that led down. He said, over his shoulder, 'Our station's next to the mainmast. There are six of us boys on the larboard watch. We sleep below.'

'Below?'

John had seen hammocks around the gun deck, and even a makeshift partition. He had thought he'd be sleeping here.

Kerslake saw his look. 'You sleep where you can find a space, but this here's the officers' and old hands' spaces. The likes of you and me are on the orlop deck.'

He led the way down. The orlop was airless and smelt of decay. A man was swabbing the deck, but the smell seemed to be part of the ship itself.

Kerslake showed him where the anchor cable was stored – 'And that space beyond, when we're in battle, that's where the surgeon works.'

John tried to imagine it. Such a small space, no room to stand upright, let alone lie down. He shut his mind against the thought of what must happen there.

They reached the kitchen area, where a man was directing storage of supplies and others were manoeuvring barrels down into the hold. They ducked through to get out of the way – and collided with two boys chasing and jumping on each other with yells of laughter.

'Slow down, Fewings!'

Kerslake seized one of the boys and stopped him in mid-flight. The chase ended, and the boys stood panting and rosy-faced, both a year or two older than John, watching, sizing him up. John looked back warily and tried not to drop his gaze.

Kerslake introduced them: Luke Fewings, Nick Wroth.

'Two of your companions of the watch,' he said.

Fewings, slightly built and short for his age, had a malicious smile; John felt instinctively that he would be trouble. Wroth looked more friendly.

Kerslake nodded towards some space near the sail-locker where hammocks were slung.

'Stow your gear there,' he said to John. 'You're at the far end, next to Fewings.'

John tossed his bag on to the hammock.

'You boys, there!' A boatswain's mate had spotted

them. 'Get on deck. We've supplies to be carried down.'

They hurried up two flights of steps to the upper deck.

After an hour or so of carrying sacks and boxes John was exhausted and relieved to stop and eat. The evening meal that the cook slopped on to his wooden platter was a stew of fish and beans. John ate hungrily, hardly noticing the taste of the food. He could still scarcely believe he was here. The long day with all its new experiences had caught up with him, and he yawned.

Around him, music was starting up: fiddles and whistles. Playing cards, greasy and well used, were laid out on top of a barrel. John noticed that some of the other boys had gone – to bed, he supposed. He might as well go, too, he thought, and made his way to the sleeping area.

Fewings and Wroth were already in their hammocks. John swung up into his – and yelped in alarm as it gave way under him, hurling him to the deck. He got up, bruised and shaken, and heard muffled laughter from the other hammocks. The knot that had attached his hammock to a ring in the wall had been made to slip. John felt a fool, knowing that the others had set him up and were watching as he struggled to re-tie it.

Luke Fewings stirred, as if from the depths of sleep. 'Having trouble?'

'No,' said John. He tested the knot, then got in.

'Well done, volunteer-boy.'

John felt hurt, and puzzled. Surely it wasn't a matter of shame to have volunteered?

'Came with your mammy's blessing, did you?' Luke persisted. 'A bite of bread and cheese tied in a clean cloth? A flask of home-brewed ale?'

It was too close to the truth. John was silent.

From the third hammock Nick Wroth said, 'Leave him, Luke.'

They were quiet then. The other two began to breathe steadily, but John lay awake. Everything was strange: the foul smell, the creaking sounds of the ship's timbers, its movement at anchor. And the unfriendliness.

2 ❖ Thursday – Friday, 28th – 29th July 1588

'Get up, you lazy vermin! Up! On your feet!'

The harsh voice of the boatswain's mate broke into John's sleep. He struggled awake and felt the hammock pushed by a rough hand. Feet were slapping on to the deck, voices groaning. John rolled out, eyes half-shut, and staggered as the unfamiliar rocking of the ship caught him off-balance. There was pain in his shoulder from last night's fall. All around him the others were pulling on clothes.

John's shoes were missing from where he'd left them by the wall. Luke Fewings, he thought. His heart beat fast. He'd be in trouble. He knew he had to stand up to Luke. It was now or never.

He barged over to the other boy and knocked him off-balance. 'Where are my shoes?'

'Your shoes?' Luke pretended to be sleepily puzzled.

'Where are they?' John tipped up Luke's hammock, spilling clothes.

'Hey!' Luke shoved him aside and they wrestled. John was smaller, but anger made him aggressive.

'You boys there!'

The boatswain's mate was heading their way.

Luke broke free. 'Behind the sail locker,' he said.

John retrieved his shoes. He came out last and got a blow to the ear from the boatswain's mate.

Mr Gains mustered all the boys on deck to learn their duties. John took gulps of fresh air as he came up. Seagulls swooped and cried above the fishing boats unloading on the quay. Carts rattled in the streets. But the life of the town was another world: so near, yet out of reach.

Most of the boys were to be attached to the master gunner's department. John and Luke were assigned to gun crews next to each other on the half-deck. John wished he wasn't so near Luke, but was glad he'd be on the upper decks, where he could see out and there would be no need to stoop. He was glad, too, to see that one of his crew was the big seaman he'd met yesterday. The gun captain, Mr Wyle, introduced him briskly to everyone: Coneybeare (the big man), Gidley, Bater, Tremain.

There were four guns on the half-deck, two on either side. Wyle's was to starboard. 'It's a saker,' he told John, 'a five-pounder. Your job will be to fetch the powder cartridges from the steward's room on the orlop. Nothing else. Except to keep out of our way. When you hear the order to fire, you move – over there! Do you understand?'

John nodded. 'Yes, sir.'

He felt quietly excited. The gun was smaller than those below, but it was one of the biggest on the upper decks, about nine feet long, made of bronze. He ran his hand over the rose of the House of Tudor embossed near the breech, and read the name of its maker and the date, 1571, incised into it.

Coneybeare showed John how the gun was loaded and fired. He explained each man's role.

'Mine's the worm,' he said, showing John a corkscrew on a long pole. 'That pulls out burning stuff. Then Gidley'll sponge out the barrel and we're ready to reload...'

'How long before you can fire again?'

'Three minutes.'

John was impressed. He began to fire questions.

'What's its range?'

'What battles have you been in?'

'Have you fought the Spanish before?'

Coneybeare laughed. 'You better slow down, boy, and bide a bit. You got a job to do after noon that'll take the bounce out of you.'

'What's that?'

Coneybeare and Wyle exchanged a grin.

'You'll find out.'

Later that day the boys were with one of the boatswain's mates, learning how to splice ropes, when the gunner's mate approached.

'I want the two smallest boys,' he said. He flicked his fingers at John and Luke.

They stepped forward.

'Down to the shot room,' the man ordered them.

John glanced nervously at Luke. 'Where's that?'

'On the orlop.'

As they descended, John saw that the seamen had begun to form a crouched human chain, stretching the length of the gun deck. All the shot lockers beside the guns were open and the gun captains and quarter-gunners were at their posts.

Now he understood. They were shotting the ship. Every shot locker had to be filled.

He followed Luke down.

The shot room was separated from the rest of the orlop deck by a canvas screen. Behind it, the different sizes of shot were piled in stout wooden boxes: the big 17lb balls, the chain-shot, and the diminishing sizes of smaller shot.

The yeoman in charge showed them the hatch above the shot room. There was scarcely space in it for two boys, and John realised why the smallest had been chosen.

He looked up and saw two seamen crouched ready on the deck above. 'You're to pass the shot up to the line,' the yeoman said. 'As I point to the shot you lift it and pass it up to the man above. One lifting, one passing. Get a rhythm going. Understand?'

They nodded.

John looked at the biggest shot and wondered if he could lift it, let alone raise it above shoulder level.

'You first.' The man indicated Luke, and pointed to one of the 17lb balls.

Luke lifted the ball, and the yeoman pointed to John's. John hefted it up. It was massive, and he staggered as he raised it to shoulder level and then higher – and felt the release as the man above took it from him.

Already Luke was passing up the next ball, and John bent to lift another. They established a rhythm, catching brief glimpses of each other as they bent and straightened. Luke's face grew red and shiny; his chest heaved with the exertion. John knew he must look the same. He had to struggle harder. He was smaller, and his left shoulder was still bruised and stiff from the fall from his hammock. He began to slow down and the yeoman struck him and shouted, 'Faster!'

John caught Luke's eye on him, and knew he must not give in. He feared Luke Fewings' scorn more than anything.

Both boys grunted with exertion. The shot was rough. It scraped John's hands and soon they were a mass of cuts and grazes. He kept his eye grimly on Luke, daring the other boy to mock.

The yeoman ordered a change to chain-shot, and that was worse. The shot came in pairs, which meant that the two of them had to work together. Each lifted one of the linked balls, and together they raised them to the same height, straining against the weight. John felt sweat running down his chest and back and dripping from his hair into his eyes. Luke was glistening and grim-faced.

At last from above John heard a shout, 'No more!' and the slam of locker lids. He experienced a brief moment of relief before they moved on to the 9lb demi-culverin balls. Although these were half the weight there were more of them and the flow was faster. Down, lift, up, release: the rhythm continued unabated. John's bruised shoulder began to stiffen; he felt himself slowing. The yeoman struck him again and swore, and John saw Luke watching, waiting for him to break. He shut his mind to the pain and lifted.

'No more!'

The lids slammed. The lower gun deck was finished. John saw the relief in Luke's eyes, knew that he was suffering, too, and felt less of a weakling himself.

Now came the lighter shot, the 5lb and 4lb balls. The smaller weight was a relief, but John was tired now, his legs had begun to shake, and both boys were panting in the airless space. As they moved on to the smallest shot, John felt his arms grow numb; his hands were smarting and slippery with blood and sweat; but still he moved at a steady pace. Each time he passed Luke he caught the other boy's eye, and knew that Luke was willing him to fail. He glared back; he wouldn't fail; he'd never give in. A battle of wills was taking place between them. John knew that if he'd been with someone sympathetic he might have collapsed by now, but the look in Luke's eyes drove him on.

'No more!'

The call was passed down the decks. It was over. John began to shake uncontrollably.

Someone reached down into the hatch and hauled him out by the shoulders. He was lifted as if he weighed nothing and carried to the upper deck and laid there to recover. Luke lay beside him, panting and drenched in sweat, his hair dripping. A seaman splashed a bucket of water over them and the cold was both a shock and a pleasure. John licked the water on his lips and tasted salt. The wind cooled him; his breathing steadied. He caught Luke's eye. The other boy nodded briefly, and John knew he'd won respect.

For the remainder of that day the boys were left much to their own devices. They watched from the upper deck as several gentleman volunteers came aboard, their servants carrying sea chests. Then came a press-gang, herding a group of dishevelled men with their hands tied behind them. Most looked resigned, but one shouted protests and was beaten with fists and cudgels as they were forced below.

'Poor devils,' said Nick. And Luke furtively raised a fist in solidarity with the one who'd fought back.

But John felt little sympathy for them. His heart was with the volunteers. He had caught the atmosphere on the ship: a feeling of expectancy.

The Armada was on its way.

It was Friday afternoon when at last the news came. John was on the upper deck, practising knots with the other boys, when there was a commotion, someone shouting, news flying from ship to ship: 'Enemy in sight! The Armada is sighted!'

The boys dropped their work. The boatswain's mate left them and hurried below. A buzz of talk went around.

'They're here – off the Lizard!'

John felt a leap of excitement. It was happening at last, and he would be part of it.

That night they saw the beacon lit on the Hoe – a flicker of orange in the rainy dark. All the beacons would be burning now, John thought: a line of fire that ran from Cornwall to London along the south coast. The signal would have reached the armies camped around Medway and Tilbury, and Lord Henry Seymour with his fleet at the Dover Strait. All would be ready.

As John was ready. He longed, now, for a sight of the enemy.

3 ❖ Saturday 30th July 1588

They left Plymouth on the noon tide, with squally rain blowing from the south-west. Crowds began gathering on the quay: wives, sweethearts and mothers, many of them in tears, and a crowd of townsfolk, cheering and waving.

Some of the boys gazed towards shore and waved back, but not John. His mother would have seen the beacon lit, but she could not have travelled the twenty miles to Plymouth in time to see him sail. In a way he was glad; he knew she'd cry, and he'd begged her not to come with him when he went to enlist. But now he felt a moment's sadness that he had no one to wave to.

Whistles blew and the men began assembling on deck. John ran to his station with the other boys. He looked around at the ranks of men lined up. On the half-deck were the ship's officers, the master gunner, the gentleman volunteers; below them, in the waist, the soldiers, sailors and topmen, all silent and waiting with the rain blowing in their faces.

The whistles sounded again, and the Commander

was piped aboard, and with him the Lieutenant of Soldiers. They joined the Master on the quarter-deck, and the Commander spoke to the ship's company of England's danger.

'The King of Spain has sent a great force against us. He seeks to invade our country and bring us once again under papist domination. But we fight for God and for the Queen's Grace and we will fight to the last man to ensure that no invader sets foot on England's shores…'

The men cheered. John's enthusiasm was real, and even the pressed men seemed inspired by the captain's words.

And now they were away. The wind was blowing them back on shore, so the boats were lowered and oarsmen took the galleons' anchors and dropped them ahead of the ships. Then the capstans were used to pull the ships out. John took his turn with the other boys at holding the lashings taut as the anchor cable was wound in. It was a slow business, and several hours had gone by before they were well clear of the harbour.

John went up on deck. The wind and rain struck cold as they came into the open sea. Now the topmen swarmed aloft; the sails cracked and filled, and John felt the wind bring the ship to life. His spirits rose at the sight of the great fleet around him, tacking towards the Eddystone Rock.

'Sails to windward!'

The lookout's cry caught everyone's attention.

The rain had become a fine mist, and at first it was difficult to distinguish anything, even the difference between sea and sky. Then John made out the shape of a sail, and then another, and another. A great crowding of sails. The Armada.

The boys gathered on the deck, their voices high with excitement.

'Reckon there's eighty of 'em!'

'No! A hundred!'

'More'n a hundred! Look, they're still coming...'

The sails were densely clustered; the Armada sailed in a tight bunched formation. Even through the mist John recognised the distinctive shape of the Spanish galleons with their towering forecastles. Ship after ship came out of the mist as if out of a dream. John admired their beauty even as he sensed their threat.

And for the first time he felt doubt. He looked around him at the English fleet strung out in line in front of the approaching enemy. They looked small and disorganised by contrast. How could they ever defeat such a force?

He tried to gauge the Armada's distance and the wind speed.

'Will we fight today?' he asked Nick.

'No.' Nick shook his head. 'Tomorrow. That's when we'll see action.'

By evening, when the whistles summoned them to eat, it was still raining and the wind blew from the west. Lord Howard had ordered the fleet to take in sail.

There was an atmosphere of tension on board. Everyone knew that the morning would bring confrontation. The boys were excited, shouting and boasting.

'We'll beat the filthy Dons!'

'Blast them out of the Channel!'

'No! We'll capture a galleon! Steal their gold.'

'They say the Spanish captains eat off plates of solid gold,' said one of the older boys.

'Their captains are so weighed down with gold chain they'd go straight to the bottom if they fell overboard!'

Nick mimicked a Spanish musketeer flourishing his weapon. 'All feathers and *fol-de-rols*, they be.'

The others laughed, and John joined in. He was beginning, at last, to feel a sense of comradeship with the group.

One of the men brought out a fiddle and began to play a rousing tune. Tremain joined in on a whistle, and the rest sang, encouraging the boys to join in. John liked singing, and he knew the words; his father had taught him. At home they'd sung sea-shanties for the joy of singing, but now the patriotic words made him feel braver.

The music was still in his head when he lay down to sleep. He hadn't slept much the last few nights, and he was tired. He fell asleep at once, but woke frequently, disturbed by the unfamiliar rolling sensation of the ship under way, and aware of a murmur of voices and the rattle of dice. And then he woke because the movement of the ship felt different.

He saw the gleam of Luke's eyes in the darkness; he'd felt it, too, and woken.

'We've altered course,' said Luke. 'Reckon we'll be to windward of the Dons by morning. Then you can show us all how brave you are, volunteer-boy.'

4 ❖ Sunday 31st July 1588

Luke was right. At dawn, when they stumbled sleepily on deck with the boatswain's mate's curses in their ears, they saw that overnight Lord Howard had led the fleet right around the approaching Armada. They were now close behind it, and had stolen the wind from its sails.

John stared in awe at the enemy fleet, at the high gilded castles, the red and gold pennants rippling from the masts, the standards with their papist images: the Virgin and Christ-child; the saints, gold-haloed. He saw the massed ranks of soldiers crowding the decks, the glint of light on muskets. He could not distinguish individual faces, but he imagined them: dark, cruel, ruthless men – the men who had killed his father. He knew that on board those ships they carried instruments of torture. He had seen a pamphlet handed out in the street in Salcombe about Spanish plans for the invasion of England. It showed two different kinds of whip, each more vicious than any English whip, and a great stock of halters to hang anyone who resisted.

If I could kill just one of them, he thought, it would avenge my father's death.

'You boys!'

A gunner's mate called them. Barrels of sand were being brought up, and all the decks were to be sprinkled to make them less slippery. Some of the men were hauling tubs of water on deck, and the carpenters were assembling their stores of tools, oakum and pitch ready for emergency repairs. Screens of netting were fixed in place to protect those on deck from falling spars.

John, scattering sand on the forecastle deck, came upon one of the gentleman volunteers leaning on the side and looking out at the Armada. He began to retreat, nervous of throwing sand too near, but the young man saw him and moved.

'Sorry, sir,' said John.

'No! I stand in your way.' He watched as John sanded the space. He was young, perhaps only eighteen or so, dressed in a sober but fine black velvet doublet with slits that showed the white linen beneath. An earring gleamed in his right ear and he wore a sword in a gilded scabbard.

'I was watching for the challenge,' he said. 'Look! There it goes!' He pointed.

John squinted into brightening daylight. A small

ship had left the *Ark Royal* with an officer standing on board and was sailing straight for the Armada.

'The *Disdain*,' said the young man. He laughed. 'She's well named.'

John guessed that all eyes from both fleets must now be on the English ship as she crossed the stretch of water between them.

He saw a billow of smoke and heard a distant explosion. The *Disdain* had fired a single shot towards the enemy. It was the signal for war to begin.

The boatswain's whistle shrilled. John hurried to his gun crew on the half-deck and was immediately sent below to fetch the first cartridge. He ran down two decks to the steward's room on the orlop. The yeoman handed him the paper cartridge; he put it in the safety case and was back in less than two minutes.

They all watched as the standards and pennants were hoisted: the cross of St George from the fore and mizzen tops, and from the main mast the royal standard – blue and red and bearing the lions and *fleur-de-lis*. Through the fleet's network of masts and rigging John saw the Armada begin to change its formation. Like a great bird, it opened wide wings. The division headed by the flagship remained in the centre, but the vanguard and rearguard moved out, one to either side, to create the fleet's battle-array: a crescent formation with trailing horns.

'Must be more'n two mile wide,' murmured Coneybeare. He whistled under his breath in admiration. 'They do keep fine formation, those Dons.'

Now the order came to make ready. Wyle placed the cartridge in a ladle and inserted it into the muzzle of the gun, followed by wadding, shot and more wadding. Bater handed him the rammer and he pushed it hard down the muzzle. Soldiers, armed with pikes and muskets, were moving into place, some nearby on the half- and quarter-decks, others in the waist, crouched inside protective coils of rope or hidden behind cloth screens strung along the sides.

John looked across the water, and saw activity on all the ships. He imagined the Spaniards making ready, too, and began to feel light-headed with a mixture of eagerness and fear.

The *Fortune* was still some way from the action when John heard the first shots reverberate across the water. The gunners watched and listened intently.

'They'm slow to return fire,' said Coneybeare, with satisfaction.

John stared out at the far-off action, longing to be involved.

He hadn't long to wait. By the time the *Fortune* reached the turmoil around the rearguard wing of the Armada the air was thick with smoke and it was difficult to see the enemy ships. The thunder of the English fleet's guns could be heard all around.

From the quarter-deck the Lieutenant of Soldiers shouted, 'Unstop your ports!'

Bater opened the gun port.

'Run out your pieces!'

As the men hauled on the ropes, John saw that they were approaching broadside on to a large galleon.

'Now be ready!' the Lieutenant warned, and Wyle signalled to John to fetch two more cartridges. Several boys jostled together on the steps as they ran down to the gun deck and then down another flight to the orlop.

John returned in time to hear the order, 'Sakers give fire!'

Wyle pushed in the priming iron and filled the touch hole with powder from his horn.

'Stand back!'

'Fire!'

The explosion sent the massive gun carriage hurtling back against the ropes and filled the air with black choking smoke. John coughed and his eyes streamed.

Dimly he watched the crew move with practised ease. Coneybeare thrust the worm down the length of the gun and jerked out bits of smouldering paper. Gidley pushed in the sponge and turned it around. Wyle cleared the touch hole. Then came the next charge and shot. Bater passed Wyle the rammer, and as it was pulled out the captain signalled for the gun to be hauled forward.

'Stand back! Fire!'

John ran for more powder. As he came back up, a ball from the Spanish ship landed short of the *Fortune*'s side, sending up a great spray of water that sluiced the deck.

Wyle's gun fired again, and through the smoke John heard distant shouting.

He handed the cartridges to Wyle, and a minute later was running below once more. He met Nick on the second ladder and they exchanged grins. The swift process of load, reload and fire was exhilarating. And they were part of it; part of the team.

'Stand back! Fire!'

The crew moved in a haze of smoke. John heard shouts and explosions but could see little except brief glimpses of sail or looming hull. At last the enemy ship moved out of range and the order came to cease fire.

'Well done, lad,' said Wyle.

It was over, then, for the moment.

'Will we go in closer, sir?'

Wyle shook his head. 'You see how their ships keep scarce fifty paces apart? Lord Howard has much respect for the Duke's formation and the strength of his ships. He won't risk it. Not yet.'

Suddenly it was action again. This time they fired several broadsides and John felt the vibration of the big guns from the deck below. Spanish shot was hitting the water all around. The smoke was foul and choking.

'You think it's bad here,' Coneybeare said, during another brief respite. 'Imagine what it's like for those poor devils. The wind's blowing it all their way.' And he laughed.

It was true. Great clouds of smoke were billowing across the water towards the Spanish ships.

The order to fire came again.

A ball glanced off the *Fortune*'s side and John heard screams. He turned, shocked, to see Tremain with his hands to his face and blood streaming between his fingers.

Coneybeare caught hold of Tremain and prised the clutching fingers apart. 'Splinter,' he said. 'No harm to the eyes.'

'Tremain, go below,' ordered Wyle. 'John – powder!'

John ran.

The gunners changed to chain-shot and aimed at the enemy's rigging. There was a cheer when the *Revenge* brought down a spar. Then, out of the smoke, John saw three great ships from the centre of the Armada coming to the aid of the outliers.

He felt the increase of tension as the gunners reloaded. All around them ships were firing. Shot plunged into the sea, sending up columns of water. A ball whistled through the yards above John's head. The smoke stung his eyes. Tremain returned with his right cheek roughly stitched.

All day John ran up and down, with only brief lulls when he could catch his breath or take a swig of beer. In the late afternoon the sea grew rough. He felt the deck rolling under his feet, and sea and sky darkened to slate-grey. Soon it was difficult to control the gun carriage, and with the light fading came the order to cease fire. John was exhausted but buzzing with excitement.

The men began clearing the decks. As John swept up shot and debris he heard the crump of a distant explosion. Everyone paused and turned towards the source of the sound: the Spanish fleet. Faintly, across the water, they heard screams and shouting, but there was nothing to be seen for the smoke.

''Tisn't one of ours,' said Gidley dismissively.

They went below for a hasty meal of ship's biscuit and cheese.

Coneybeare dropped a hand on John's shoulder. 'You did well, boy.'

His praise warmed John.

'It was exciting!'

'We'll see some more action tomorrow,' said Coneybeare.

5 ❖ Monday – Saturday, 1st – 6th August 1588

But there was no fighting the next day.

After a night of heavy seas the *Fortune* found herself isolated. In the distance could be seen other English ships, but none within hailing distance. The fleet was scattered. Far off John saw the Armada, in tight formation, moving steadily away up-Channel.

'It'll take most of the day to regroup,' said Wyle.

John was disappointed. He'd liked being with the gun crew; he'd felt useful and gained their approval. Now he was with the boys again. They assembled on the upper deck for training with the boatswain.

Kerslake arrived full of news.

'That explosion we heard yesterday – remember? One of the Dons' ships blew up!'

They all cheered.

'The powder magazine?' asked Nick.

'So it seem. Blew the whole stern off. Near two hundred dead. And scores burnt.'

The boys laughed, jumped and rolled about, mimicking the explosion, and the men thrown into the sea.

Mr Gains called them to order. 'You should be ashamed,' he said.

'But they're our enemies, sir,' Kerslake said.

'They are. But it could have happened to any ship,' said Gains. 'A spark, that's all it takes. Any ship,' he repeated. 'Spanish or English.'

Luke pulled a face behind the man's back, and John smiled. The shared mockery brought them together – but only for a moment.

'You'll be going aloft today,' said Mr Gains. 'Get you young ones used to climbing.'

John looked up at the alarming network of yards and rigging and straining canvas.

'Amery!'

John jumped. 'Sir?'

'Go with Kerslake. The rest of you pair up...' He gave instructions and sent them away. 'Kerslake, see how the lad climbs. If he's able, take him up to the main topsail.'

John had been learning the names of the sails. The lowest sail on the main mast was the mainsail. The main topsail was the one above it. It looked impossibly high – and yet, he thought, it must be good to be up there, above the squalor of the ship, among gulls and clouds.

Kerslake led John to the rope netting that ran up

from the side. 'You go first,' he said.

The broad netting was easy to climb. John swung up readily. As he climbed higher he began to feel more and more nervous. The wind caught and wrestled with his hair and clothes, the ship rolled, the great sail strained in the wind, and he saw the deck moving far below. John wondered how the deck could hold the weight of all the masts and rigging.

He reached the yard from which the mainsail was hung, and then, with relief, the platform at the base of the topsail.

'Well done.' Kerslake came up panting beside him.

They looked out to sea. The fleet was still scattered, separated by miles of choppy water. Great waves tilted the deck of the *Fortune* far below, and John realised how small the galleon was in the vastness of the sea.

'The Armada must be near Portland Bill now.' Kerslake pointed out the distant Spanish fleet.

'Will they try to take the Isle of Wight?'

Kerslake shrugged. 'My gun crew are saying they'll aim to sail up the Thames. They've got an army waiting in Dunkirk. They'll join forces – make for London.'

The sea was rougher still when Mr Gains called them down. As the ship pitched and rolled, John began to feel panicky. I can't do it, he thought. Kerslake went first, and John struggled to follow him off the platform. The sails cracked and tightened, and the plunging of the ship made him afraid to let go. He reached the mainsail yard and clung, terrified. He knew he couldn't move again.

Kerslake looked up. 'Trouble?'

'I can't – can't…'

'Yes, you can. Just take one hand off, and move down.'

John saw the deck, with tiny figures on it, pitching below him.

'I can't.'

Kerslake came back up. 'I'll help.'

But John couldn't move. He was rigid with fear.

Kerslake said, 'I'm right below you. You can't fall. Now move your right hand and foot. Don't look down.'

But John did, and saw Mr Gains waiting.

The sight of the boatswain scared him into action. He let go, felt his weight drag, grabbed the netting lower down. Now the left side. He was moving. Terrified, but moving.

'That's good,' said Kerslake. 'And again…'

It seemed to take for ever, but at last John scrambled down the last few yards and landed, shaken, to find the whole company of boys assembled on the deck and watching him.

'You're slow, Amery,' said Mr Gains.

Tears of shame sprang to John's eyes, and he bit his lip and looked down – but not before he'd seen the smirk on Luke Fewings' face.

'It gets easier,' Kerslake said later. John was grateful. Kerslake had been kinder than he'd expected. But John was furious with himself for being afraid, and for letting Luke see it.

Luke took full advantage. At every opportunity he remarked on John's failure. 'Going up to the gun deck, John? Be careful. You might not be able to get down again.' And, at the end of the watch, 'Oh! He's managed to climb into his hammock!'

The others showed casual sympathy.

'Don't mind Luke,' said Nick, as they ate together the next day. 'He'll get tired of it in the end.'

'But why does he hate me?' asked John.

'He doesn't. It's the shipboard life he hates.'

'Did the press-gang take him?'

'Aye. Both of us were taken in Plymouth – must be two year ago now. I've spent scarce twelve weeks ashore since.'

John began to understand – he'd volunteered for a life that Luke hated. But it's no excuse, he thought; no reason to take it out on me.

'Where have you been?' he asked Nick.

'Spain. Panama … that was on the *Enterprise*. Porto Rico…'

'*Porto Rico!*' John felt envious. I could like this life, he thought, if it wasn't for Luke Fewings.

It was cold on deck that day. A brisk wind blew from the north-east, giving the advantage to the Armada. John saw that a skirmish was taking place off the Isle of Wight, but the *Fortune* was not involved. Tremain played tunes on a whistle, and Coneybeare sat leaning against a gun carriage, deftly knotting a string bag in fancy patterns. A pocket, he called it, for his wife.

The boys all got together for a game of fox and hounds, hiding and chasing each other up and down ladders and rigging, around the guns, in and out of the hatches. John enjoyed running with the hounds, though he avoided the rigging for fear of Luke's mockery; but later, when he was the fox, he felt threatened and was relieved when Mr Gains called them away for more work with knots.

All that week the English fleet followed the Armada up-Channel. There were a few battles, but the *Fortune*'s part in them was brief, and John spent more time under the boatswain's instruction, or being baited by Luke Fewings. Luke, having discovered John's weakness, would not let go; he buzzed around his victim like a fly.

Everyone on the ship was bad-tempered. The gunners complained of a shortage of ammunition, and the whole ship's company complained about the beer, which was sour and turned the stomach. John had even tried drinking water instead, but it was slimy, and he knew water was dangerous stuff.

They had endured the beer while they were engaged in battle, but now the men were getting angry.

Gidley, always quick to complain, held forth on the orlop deck, well away from any officers. 'Only a week at sea and we run out of shot! Food's getting short. The beer's sour. They let themselves be swindled by the victuallers and they let the Duke of Medina Sidonia sail up the English Channel without—'

'Quiet, man!' snapped Wyle. 'You could hang for such talk.'

But men nodded agreement. And John felt cheated, too. He had come to fight the Spanish, to drive them away from England's shores, and here they were, a week later, still following the Armada up-Channel towards Kent, and they'd had no more effect on its progress than a dog nipping at ankles.

He found Coneybeare on the upper deck and asked him, 'Why don't the commanders *do* something?'

'Can't do nothing without shot, can they?' said Coneybeare comfortably; he was at his knotting again.

'But they'm sending more, I heard. From the two ships we captured that first day. When will it come?'

'Tomorrow, they reckons. Don't hurry it on, boy. Remember the work you had last time? It's not for the likes of us to worry about.'

John saw the other boys signalling to him. They wanted to play fox and hounds again.

'You're the fox – remember?' said Luke.

The others counted fifty. John ran.

Where? Down below? No. There were plenty of hiding places, but he'd be cornered. He ran up on deck, hid in one of the coils of rope used by the soldiers, crouched down small.

The pack went by, hallooing. He stayed hidden as they circled the deck. Footsteps came near. He raised his head, and Nick gave cry, 'The fox! The fox!'

John scrambled out. Nick blocked the way down, and there was nowhere to go except up the rigging.

It was a mistake. Luke came up fast behind him. 'Don't go too high,' he taunted. 'Us might have to come and rescue you.'

John kicked out, furious. He'd had enough of this.

Luke grabbed his ankle. 'You're caught! Fox is caught! Can he get down, though?' He began a mocking imitation of Kerslake: 'Take it steady, now. One step at a time. Don't look down...'

'Hold your gab!' shouted John. He let go, slithered, and landed on Luke, pulling the two of them down together. They rolled on to the deck, fighting. At once the other boys formed a circle around them. Luke was stronger, but John had a week's anger in him. He hurled himself at Luke, raining punches. Luke fought back, hitting hard, but John slammed into him again and knocked him down. The other boys yelled with excitement. John seized Luke by the hair and began banging his head on the deck.

'Leave him!'

It was Mr Wyle. The onlookers scattered. Wyle seized John, yanked him to his feet. Luke got up slowly, and John was shocked to see blood streaming from his nose and a bruise already swelling on his cheekbone. His own knuckles were skinned but he seemed otherwise unhurt.

'We've an enemy to fight,' said Wyle, 'and we need you boys fit and fast. No injuries.' He turned to John with a look of angry bewilderment. 'What's got into you?'

'Sorry, sir.'

'You will be. Boatswain'll likely put you in the hold to cool down.'

'Sorry, sir.' John knew he was in trouble now. Mr Gains would have no mercy on him.

Luke's lip was split. He spoke with difficulty, dabbing at the trickling blood. 'Don't report him, sir. It was me. I've been asking for it. Truly.'

John looked up, astonished. Wyle stared from one to another of them. Then he gave John a shake. 'All right. But no more chances. Understood? Now get yourselves cleaned up. We'll be off the Kent coast soon. There's a war to fight.'

He strode away.

John looked at Luke. 'Thanks,' he said.

Luke merely shrugged and turned to go below, but John sensed that a truce had been declared.

On Saturday some of the captured Spanish shot

was brought out from the Sussex coast, along with supplies of food and water. Once again John and Luke had the task of passing up the shot, but there was less to do this time. Luke hadn't said much since the fight, but he had stopped tormenting John. And John didn't mind the work; he felt that something was happening at last. There was a feeling of expectancy. Carpenters could be seen on the sides of the *Revenge*, making repairs. The enemy was less than two miles away, and everyone was tense now, waiting to see what they would do as they approached the Straits of Dover.

Before long it was clear that they were sailing for Calais. The fleet followed them. By late afternoon the Armada had anchored several miles off Calais, and the English fleet anchored, too. 'No more'n a culverin-shot away,' said Wyle, with satisfaction.

In the lull that followed, Mr Gains took the opportunity to send the younger boys aloft for some more training. John managed better this time. And it was while they were there that the lookout sighted sails off to the north-west. The Dover contingent was on its way, with thirty-five ships.

A cheer rose up. Men came running from below and crowded the decks. Everyone shouted, and a couple of men danced a jig. John saw movement on all the ships and heard cheering throughout the fleet.

We have the Dons now, he thought. They can't escape.

6 ❖ Sunday 7th August 1588

John leaned on the ship's side, looking out at the enemy fleet. The rain had eased, and the last rays of sunset caught the Armada's rigging and lit up the galleons as if they were on fire.

It was past the end of John's watch, and he should have been below in his hammock, but he had been drawn by the faint sound of singing drifting across the water from the Armada. From time to time a shift in the wind direction would bring the sound towards him more strongly. Now, for a moment, he caught the full strength of thousands of men's voices raised in song.

The Litany. John realised that he was hearing the sound of the enemy fleet at evening prayer – all of them together, every ship, every man. The power of their singing moved him, and for the first time John understood that they believed in their cause, and trusted in God, just as he did. They believed they were bringing the true faith back to England.

He saw that they had moved a line of small ships, like a defensive screen, in front of the galleons.

In both fleets there had been activity all day. He'd seen boats coming and going from the galleons to the *Ark Royal*; not only the squadron leaders, but the captains of some of the lesser ships had been summoned.

'There's the *Thomas*'s boat going out,' Kerslake had said, when they were aloft on the main topgallant yard under the eye of Mr Gains.

'What are they planning, do you think?' asked John.

'Fireships, I'd reckon.'

Fireships! John felt a shiver of excitement.

They'd both looked out across the water at the massed sails of the Armada, anchored and waiting.

'When?'

'When the wind and tide's right.'

The wind's right now, thought John, but not the tide; not for a few hours. He thought of the Spanish sailors, singing prayers to God, and imagined the terror to come.

Below, on the orlop, the other boys were already in their hammocks. John rolled into his. The four-hour watches had kept him constantly tired, and he slept at once.

'John! Wake up!'

Kerslake was shaking him.

It was dark, dead of night, and John's eyes didn't want to open, but he heard the boatswain's whistle and the mate's shouts and knew it was time.

He heard other sounds, too: men's voices out on the water, an anchor being raised.

The fireships! He rolled out, and groped for his clothes. Men were hurrying up the ladders to the upper deck. Here and there a lantern cast a flicker of light on faces as they emerged into the cold midnight air.

The ships were about to be launched. There were eight of them, small warships prepared for sacrifice, and filled with anything that would burn: rope, wood, canvas, pitch. Their cannons were loaded and would fire when the heat reached them. A few men were at work aboard each one, and more in rescue boats alongside.

'Volunteers,' said Kerslake. 'They'll get a shilling each. I wanted to go, but they'm not taking boys.'

John looked across at the Armada and saw movement there. They'd been expecting this, he guessed.

At a signal, all eight ships were cast loose.

They went fast, carried by the wind and a strong tide. About halfway across the dark space of water the first burst of flame appeared at the prow of one of the ships. The others quickly followed. Within minutes all the ships were ablaze. Flames raced up the rigging, outlining in fire the shape of each ship. The sails caught and blazed, and streamed behind the yards like burning flags. And then the guns began to fire. Smoke and flame poured from the gun ports and fierce fire burned from prow to stern.

The men cheered. Everyone was on deck, watching and commenting.

'See how they go! What a speed!'

'Tide's fast!'

'They got a line of ships there, with grappling hooks—'

'That won't stop 'em.'

But John could see that the first two fireships had been caught by the hooks and pulled aside, away from the fleet. The next got through, followed by the others, drawn by wind and tide towards the heart of the Armada.

The *Fortune*'s crew yelled and cheered as the Spanish galleons began to cut their cables and flee. Shouts and cries of panic came faintly across the water.

Coneybeare had appeared next to John. He was laughing. 'Look at that!' he said with relish. 'Perfect timing! Perfect! Those galleons, they'll all have two, maybe three, anchors out tonight. They'll lose 'em all. And see how they go! Fleeing like sheep!'

It was difficult, now, to see what was happening. The fireships were burning lower, and only a confused sense of movement could be seen. But it was clear that the Armada would be scattered by morning.

The men returned to their stations and began to prepare for battle. John fetched the first powder cartridge for Wyle. When he came back on deck he saw that the fireships had burned out and the boats were returning with the volunteers. Two were from the *Fortune*. One came aboard drenched; he'd had to leap into the sea. Both were scorched and smoke-stained, but they arrived to cheers and went below, boasting of their adventure.

John yawned as he listened to the men's talk. He sat leaning against a coil of rope and felt his eyelids drooping. He struggled to stay awake; there could be terrible punishments for sleeping on watch. But Wyle saw him and put a hand on his shoulder. 'Don't fear to sleep. I'll wake you when you're needed.'

'Will we chase 'em, sir?'

'Aye. We'll chase 'em right back to their orange groves. When dawn breaks we'll be ready.'

7 ❖ Monday 8th August 1588: Dawn

The cold woke John; cold and rain. He opened his eyes to a grey dawn. He was still on deck, his cheek pressed against the harsh fibres of the coiled rope, his body stiff and cold. He remembered the events of last night, stumbled to his feet, and saw the gunners talking and looking out to sea. He squeezed in among them; saw grey sea, grey sky, a scattered sail or two. 'They're gone!' he said. 'Gone – all but a few...'

The flagship was there, the *San Martin*, and four other big galleons. Towards Calais another lay wrecked on a sandbank, and in the distance, some as far away as the horizon, were the ships of the Armada. Buoys bobbed on the water, marking the anchors they had left behind.

Wyle laughed. 'Well, we've five of them here against our whole fleet. It'll be hours before the Duke gets them all back together.' He turned to John, whose teeth were chattering. 'Boy, you're turning blue! We'll be weighing anchor soon. Go below and get some food while there's time.'

John and Luke went down together into the warm stink of the orlop deck. The cooking fire would not be lit today, but they ate ship's biscuits and cheese, washed down with sour beer.

The men were in fighting mood. They predicted driving the remnants of the Armada on to the sandbanks of Flanders.

'That'll be what his Lordship aims to do. They got nowhere to go, have they? It's us, or the shallows.'

'Aye, we'll litter the Flanders beaches with Spanish ships.'

'And be home by Friday!'

They laughed.

Luke glanced towards the men and rolled his eyes upwards. 'Home!' he said. It sounded contemptuous.

'Don't you want to go home?' John asked.

'Nowhere to go. Not like you, Johnny-boy. I was living on the streets when the press-gang took me.'

'Your mother…?'

'Dead. And dead drunk before that. Never knew my father.'

John thought of his own home at Hope, his mother and sister, the memory of his father. He'd have been a different kind of person without them.

The order came to weigh anchors, and John and Luke were sent to help. When the whistles blew, summoning all to their stations, John felt his stomach curdling – whether from the beer or from tension he was not sure. He ran to join his gun crew, and saw Luke already at the next saker.

The decks had been sanded, the tubs of water and the carpenters' tools placed ready. Net screens overhead protected the ship from boarders. He heard the sound – familiar, now – of the sails being hoisted, and looked up at their crowding mass above him. The wind was blowing towards the Flanders sandbanks. John saw, far in the distance, Lord Howard's squadron already moving towards the stricken ship on the Calais shore. But the *Fortune* was in Drake's squadron, and Drake's target was the Spanish duke's flagship. The *Revenge* led the attack, and the English galleons, the *Fortune* among them, followed.

'Powder!' yelled Wyle – and John's work had begun. He fetched the first cartridge, and as the crew loaded the gun he watched an exchange of fire between the *Revenge* and the *San Martin*. The *Revenge* took a hit.

'Unstop your ports!' roared the Lieutenant on the quarter-deck. 'Run out your pieces!'

The crew loosed the side tackles, threw their weight on the ropes, and hauled the gun into place.

John was surprised to see how much the gap between the *Fortune* and the nearest Spanish galleon had lessened.

We're going in closer than before, he realised.

He could see the soldiers crowded on the decks in orderly ranks, each with his musket trained on them as they approached. There were marksmen on the high fore and after castles, and even in the rigging.

The distance between them narrowed to no more than a hundred yards, and closing.

'Now be ready!' shouted the Lieutenant as musket shot glanced off the hull nearby. 'All starboard pieces give fire!'

The *Fortune*'s broadside erupted in black smoke. John felt the thunder of the big guns on the deck below. Screams and shouts came across the water, and as the smoke cleared he saw that a swathe had been cut through the massed ranks of Spanish soldiers amidships. The side of the ship had shattered, exposing the bloodstained deck, the wounded men struggling to rise. A gunner lay dead across his cannon. A man clung to the broken hull with one arm; the other was a bleeding stump.

'Powder!' shouted Wyle. And John turned his back on the carnage and darted below. While he was on the gun deck he felt the shock of a Spanish broadside shake the ship, but no shot pierced the hull. When he returned it was to see black smoke billowing from the sakers' return fire.

John handed Wyle the cartridge. A musket ball hummed between the two of them and embedded itself in the mizzen mast. Instinctively, John ducked as the musketeers fired again.

'Chain-shot!' shouted the Lieutenant from above them. 'Aim for the rigging!'

Tremain and Gidley took out the wedges from beneath the gun's breech to lift its angle of fire. They hauled the gun back and Wyle pushed in the charge, wad and shot.

'All starboard pieces give fire!'

The gun recoiled, and at the same moment John felt in his bones the vibration from the cannons below. He coughed as the smoke rose. As he ran for powder he glanced back at the enemy ship. Through the clearing smoke he saw that a spar had been smashed and hung precariously above the deck, bringing the topsail with it. A man clinging to the damaged spar let go and plummeted down. Several marksmen were gone from the rigging and there was screaming and disarray among the soldiers who had been massed on the aftercastle.

The *Fortune*'s gunners cheered.

John hurried below. Because the fighting was at close range, all the smaller upper-deck guns were now in use and there were more powder boys on the move. They joked and laughed as they ran bent over in the confined space. Luke lurched down, mimicking a falling soldier.

John laughed. 'They'm slow!' he said.

'Aye – they can't return fire as fast as us.'

John put his cartridges in the case and ran back up.

The deck was thick with smoke and John couldn't see the enemy ship, though he knew from the creaking and grinding sounds and the voices of men that it was close.

'They'll get a grappling hook on us, given a chance,' said Wyle.

Soldiers crouched nearby, ready to repel boarders. Suddenly the smoke cleared and the hull of the Spanish ship loomed almost upon them. A hail of musket fire raked the deck. John scurried for the cover of his gun and gave Wyle the cartridge. He could see the Spanish sailors ready with grappling hooks.

The next shot from the *Fortune* smashed into the aftercastle of the Spanish ship, shattering wood and sending splinters flying. Men were hurled across the decks and into the sea.

Still the Spanish soldiers regrouped and returned fire. Another broadside thundered out but went wide.

'Stand clear!' shouted Wyle, and touched flame to powder. The shot struck home, smashing a great hole in the Spanish galleon's hull. John ran for powder, and when he came up again he saw the enemy ship's scuppers running with blood.

He was amazed at their desperate courage. They can't go on, he thought. They must surrender.

The saker crew was making ready when the Spanish guns fired again. One moment John was watching as Bater handed Wyle the rammer; the next, he felt a massive impact and was flung off his feet. The world seemed to explode into a chaos of splinters, screams, curses, falling bodies, dust. John hit the deck hard, face-down, and lay still for a moment, stunned and deafened.

When at last he dared to raise his head he saw that a gun had broken loose and two blood-spattered men were struggling to restrain it. Smoke and dust filled his mouth and he felt blood trickling down the side of his face. He wiped it with his hand; a cut, nothing more. He was alive. It seemed miraculous. He got to his feet slowly as the smoke cleared, and stared around.

The ball had smashed through a few feet away, hurling the crew of the next saker across the deck, and embedding itself in the aftercastle. Great jagged splinters of wood littered the deck, and among them lay men, groaning and bleeding, some still pierced with splinters. Wyle and Bater had run to help with the loose gun. Tremain appeared, dusty and bloodstained. As injured men began struggling to their feet a burst of musket fire raked the half-deck, causing them all to dive for cover.

Luke! thought John. Where's Luke? And then he saw him. Luke lay slumped against the aftercastle, all colour gone from his face, his left leg a bloody mangled mess.

'Oh, God! Luke!' cried John, and ran towards him.

'Leave him!' shouted Wyle. His voice was harsh. 'Leave him – he's gone!'

8 ❖ Monday 8th August 1588: Noon

John ignored the command. He ducked and ran doubled up as musket shot hummed around him, and flung himself down beside Luke.

'Luke...'

The boy's eyelids fluttered. He groaned.

John turned his head. 'He's alive! Mr Wyle! Help me!'

Close to, Luke's leg was a horrifying sight. It was smashed, the bone exposed, and the torn breeches and stockings were soaked with blood. John didn't know how to begin to move him.

The Spanish musketeers were still firing. In response, a group of soldiers ran across to crouch between the sakers, firing back.

John lifted Luke's arm and placed it over his own shoulder. 'Try and stand on the other leg.'

He felt Luke's hand clutch feebly at his shoulder. As he attempted to raise him, Luke screamed in pain. The bright spreading stain of blood widened rapidly and streamed down the shattered leg. John looked around, desperate. At last! Coneybeare was coming towards them.

'Leave him, boy. I'll take him.' And he hoisted Luke in his arms and carried him towards the stairway. 'Get back to your post.'

John watched them disappear below. He wanted to follow. Luke was gasping in pain at every jolt of Coneybeare's movement on the heaving deck. He looked back at John, his eyes full of fear.

'John!' yelled Wyle. 'Powder!'

The guns were in action again. John was shaking and his legs felt weak. He took the cartridge case and stumbled below, slower than he had been before. He saw men helping the other wounded gunners to safety, and remembered the space Kerslake had shown him the day he arrived: the makeshift surgeon's cabin. It was only yards from the steward's room. He thought of Luke being taken there and imagined how afraid he must be.

When he came up on deck Wyle caught him a blow on the ear that made him stagger. Wyle's face was smudged black with gunpowder and his eyes stared out, pale and angry. He rammed home the charge and then, as he returned to the breech end where John waited, he said, 'You're here to obey orders! I could have you keelhauled for what you did.'

'I'm sorry, sir.'

John felt close to tears. He wanted Wyle to be pleased with him. He wanted to be part of this team, one of them. But he couldn't have left Luke...

He blinked rapidly. To cry now would be the worst thing of all.

'Stand back!' roared Wyle.

John stood well clear.

'Fire!'

All day the battle wore on. The scattered ships of the Armada had regrouped and there was fighting all along the coast. The sea grew rough and the ship's movement made it difficult to aim the guns. John heard that one of Luke's saker crew had died. He heard nothing of Luke. Perhaps he had died, too. They'll have taken his leg off, he thought. Luke had known that; the horror of it was in his eyes when Coneybeare carried him below.

There was bitter anger towards the enemy now among the gunners and soldiers. The Armada had regained its defensive formation, but late in the afternoon the *Fortune*, along with several other galleons, managed to isolate one of the Spanish ships. Through mist and rain, as they closed in around her, John read the name on her side: *Maria Juan*. She was a bigger ship than the *Fortune*, but with fewer guns, and her hull was already damaged. They surrounded her like wolves going in for the kill and pounded her from all sides. John felt the satisfaction of every blow that struck her. With joy he saw the rigging broken by chain-shot, the soldiers cut down, the divers desperately trying to repair the hull under a barrage of fire. After two hours her flags hung in tatters and she trailed a bloody wake behind her in the sea.

Still she fought on. But a final broadside holed her below the waterline and John and the men around him cheered to see the white flag and to hear the captain call out that he surrendered.

'She'm a prize worth taking,' Bater said.

'Too late!' exclaimed Wyle. 'Look! She's going!'

John stared. Wyle was right. The *Maria Juan* had begun to heel over. Water poured in through her shattered hull and men were hurled across the overcrowded decks. John heard screams and shouts and saw how the soldiers slid and fell one on top of another, and struggled to rise again. A group of soldiers managed to launch one of the boats. John watched as it was filled and lowered. Before another could be freed the sea rushed in through the ship's gun ports and she began to sink. Men were flung from the upper decks into the sea as she heeled over and went down, sucking many of the survivors down with her and trapping all those below decks. It was over in minutes. Nothing was left but one boat-load of survivors and men struggling in the waves, crying out for help.

'God have mercy on them,' muttered Wyle.

John stood stunned. He felt a mixture of horror and satisfaction.

The sea was now so rough that fighting was abandoned. The north-westerly wind was blowing both fleets towards the sandbanks, and the *Fortune* was running out of shot. The men went below to eat, but John made his way to the surgeon's room, bracing himself for what he might see and hear there.

The canvas screen that marked off the surgeon's space was spotted with blood. John heard movement from inside and the sound of someone breathing heavily. He hesitated. 'Sir…?' he said.

The surgeon pulled back the screen. He was a big, rough-looking man with a face scarred by smallpox. His clothes were stiff with dried blood and there was blood caught in the hair of his forearms and under his fingernails. John looked past him and saw several injured men. His glance flicked over them and settled on Luke, who lay on a pallet.

The leg was gone. It had been removed below the knee, which was tightly bandaged and showed a red stain coming through. His face was papery white, the eyes dark-shadowed, and it was his loud breathing that John had heard. His eyes focused on John, but he seemed only half-awake.

'Your friend?' the surgeon asked.

For a second John hesitated. Then he said, 'Yes, sir.'

'We make 'em drunk,' the man explained, 'to dull the pain. He's had a draught of opium, too.'

John looked at Luke, then back at the surgeon. He didn't dare ask what he wanted to know.

'It's safer than musket shot or a splinter wound,' the man said. 'Nothing left behind to fester.'

The surgeon began packing away implements: bowls, needles, a saw with dried blood in its teeth. A heap of blood-stained rags lay on the table and he swept them into a leather bucket.

'What happened to him, sir? I never saw.'

'Gun broke loose. Pinned him against the cabin wall. Fetch your mate – the big fellow. He can carry the lad to his hammock.'

John went to join the rest of his crew who were already eating. He felt no appetite for the cold bacon and hard biscuit, but he ate it because

Coneybeare told him to, and felt better for it afterwards.

Coneybeare went with John to fetch Luke, who groaned when they moved him, but afterwards lay quietly in his hammock. John stayed watching for a while, but when Luke drifted off to sleep he left him and went up on deck, feeling angry and miserable on his behalf.

Some boys were leaning on the side, looking out to sea, talking and pointing. Curiosity drew him towards them.

'Look!' said one of them, with a grin. 'Out there!'

John looked out at the heaving sea. The Armada was anchored some way off, but a boy – a survivor, he supposed, from the *Maria Juan* – was clinging to a piece of wreckage near the *Fortune*.

'*Socorro!*'

They heard the boy's cries, faint in the wind and rain.

'*Socorro!*'

The sea brought the boy closer to the ship. He was losing his struggle. Great waves occasionally submerged him, then tossed him up again. John saw the tight clutch of his fingers on the broken spar.

The boy caught their gaze on him and looked up

at them, crying out in desperation, '*Socorro! Por el amor de Dios!*'

The *Fortune*'s boys jeered. John felt a surge of hatred against the unknown boy.

'Drown, you papist dog!' he shouted. 'Drown – and be damned!'

The others looked at him in some surprise, then added a few oaths of their own. But John cared nothing for their company. He turned his back on them and went below.

An hour later he was back on deck, helping to sweep and clear debris. It was raining and an early dusk darkened sea and sky. He looked out and saw the broken spar from the *Maria Juan* rising and falling on the swell. The boy was gone.

To his surprise John felt grief overwhelm him. He took himself away from the others and swept vigorously to hide his feelings, but he could not stem the flow of tears. He rubbed a dirty hand across his face, not understanding. Who was he crying for? Luke? The dead gunner? His father? Not the boy from the *Maria Juan*. No Spanish boy deserved his tears.

9 ❖ August–September 1588

'I won't die, will I?'

It was a day since the amputation, and John had managed to persuade Luke to sit up and drink some broth.

'No! Surgeon said it's clean.'

'I saw a man die, once, from a wound that went foul. Days, he lingered.' Luke's face looked pinched and sunken. 'The pain's bad.'

'I'll ask if you can have more opium.'

John sat with Luke whenever he was free. There was no more fighting. Last night it had seemed that God was on England's side and that the Spanish fleet would be wrecked on the sandbanks of Flanders. But today the wind had changed, blowing the Armada into the North Sea. The Plymouth squadrons had set off in pursuit.

'We'm just putting on a brag,' said Coneybeare. 'Seeing them off. Shot lockers are almost empty.'

Away from Luke, John asked Coneybeare, 'That wound won't fester, will it?'

'Let's hope not. It does happen. But the lad's

young ... We must pray, John.'

After a few anxious days Luke's colour improved and the pain lessened. Coneybeare carried him up on deck for some air. 'You'm a lightweight,' he said. 'Lighter than I was,' agreed Luke. John thought: if he can make a joke surely he'll survive. Later that day Luke managed to get out of the hammock with John's help and hobbled around the deck, his fingers digging hard into John's shoulder. He was exhausted afterwards, but the next day he got out again, and the two of them struggled to the upper deck, where they laughed as the rain and wind forced them to take shelter. In the distance they saw the ships of the Armada.

'Where are we?' Luke asked.

'Off the Firth of Forth, I think.'

'It's blowing up a gale.'

'Aye. Coneybeare reckons we'll turn for home tonight. He says with this wind behind them the Dons will have to sail right round Scotland and Ireland and then home to Spain.'

'We've beat 'em, then.'

'Seems so.'

The ship's carpenter made crutches for Luke, but as the gales grew stronger and the ship rolled in massive seas it was easier for Luke to get about holding on to John. All down the east coast of England the fleet battled against storms, and the men had to endure a dwindling, rotting food supply and the usual sour beer.

Then sickness broke out and spread rapidly through all the ships.

John felt queasy one morning and within hours he was burning hot and retching. By evening he was delirious.

Afterwards, he had confused memories of those times. For days – he didn't know how many – he lay exhausted in his own mess and vomit. His clothes stank and he was unable to eat or even to lift his head without faintness. Familiar faces came and went: Luke, Wyle, Coneybeare. He became aware that men were dying, that there were scarcely enough fit to sail the ship, let alone care for those who were ill.

'Kerslake's gone,' Coneybeare told him, 'and Bater. And several of the topmen.' There were tears on his cheeks.

John felt so ill he thought he would die, too. But he began to recover, and one day he heard gulls and knew from the motion of the ship that they were at anchor.

'We've reached Margate,' said Coneybeare.

'They'm putting us all ashore here.'

It was only when he saw the men, sick and starving, stumbling ashore at Margate, that John realised what a disaster had overtaken the fleet. He was thin and weak, and the rolling gait he'd become used to on the ship wouldn't serve him now. Luke's face was gaunt as he hobbled on his crutches. But they were the lucky ones; some were so frail they fell and died in the street.

John, Luke and some of the gunners found lodgings in a barn and outhouses attached to the Anchor Inn on the Canterbury road. All were discharged on half pay. There was no money, it seemed, in the Treasury, and Lord Howard paid many of the men out of his own pocket.

As August turned to September Luke and John helped out at the inn and slowly recovered their strength. Luke had a wooden leg made and soon began to adapt to it. They talked to each other about their lives. John told Luke about playing on the beach and cliffs at Hope, about helping the fishermen, about his father and the voyage they'd made to Flanders on the *Pearl*. Luke had been a street child, a thief, living by his wits. They could not have been more different, John thought, and yet a bond had grown between them that would be hard to break.

But the West Country men were all beginning to drift homewards, and John was eager to go, too.

'Come with me,' he said to Luke.

'Me? With this peg-leg?'

'We'll get a boat. Work our passage.'

But Luke was settled at the inn, washing pots, lighting fires, feeding the animals, and telling stories of his adventures to the kitchen maids. He'd never wanted to go to sea and he had no ties in Plymouth. They wouldn't meet again, John realised.

He set off west with Coneybeare and Gidley. They walked to Southampton, sleeping under hedges or in barns, and paid their way by helping out with the harvest. In the town they heard of the Queen's victory celebrations in London. 'No want of money there,' said Gidley bitterly. 'No lack of honours and knighthoods and fine clothes. But we go home without our pay.'

They heard, too, of God's wrath: Spanish ships wrecked in Scotland and all down the west coast of Ireland – dozens of great galleons, the glory of Spain.

In Southampton they got a passage on a merchant ship that brought them into Salcombe in late September. And from there John walked home.

10 ❖ Wednesday 6th November 1588

John woke to the roar of wind and the crashing of waves. For a moment he thought he was back on board the *Fortune*, battling against gales in the North Sea. Then he remembered: he was home, the Armada campaign was behind him, and it was his mother's cottage in Hope Cove that was battling as the wind penetrated every crack to shake the hangings and rattle doors and loose boards. He heard the sea crashing on the Shippen Rock and dragging back down the beach with a grating of pebbles. And he heard voices: distant voices, half-drowned by the keening of the wind, and others close by, urgent and eager.

'John! John!'

It was Kate.

His sister burst into the room. She had dressed hurriedly and was fastening her bodice as she talked.

'There's a wreck!' Her eyes glittered with excitement. 'On the Shippen. A Spanish galleon.'

John sprang up.

'Spanish?'

'Aye. From the Armada, they'm saying.'

'It can't be...' So long, so many months? John began pulling on clothes over his night-shift.

Their mother would not come. 'It'll be all looting and cruelty,' she said. 'Turns folk into beasts.'

But John and Kate went out into the square and followed the people hurrying to the beach. It was not yet dawn, but the sky was lightening, the moon pale with ragged clouds flying across it.

The tide was half in and the beach was full of people. A boat had come ashore, and men with sea chests were struggling out of it. But John's eyes were drawn beyond them, out to sea – to the wreck. It had struck the line of small rocks that ran out from the base of the Shippen. The bowsprit and part of the hull were smashed and the ship had heeled over and was already half-submerged.

But even in that grey morning light John knew her for a ship of the Armada. The high forecastle, patterned in red and gold, the Spanish flags, and the men: the men who struggled ashore were mostly musketeers and pikemen like those he'd fought off the banks of Flanders.

He brought his attention back to the beach. Men were coming ashore and falling exhausted, face down, on the stones. Their clothes were in tatters, soaked and filthy, their hair matted. When one of them lifted his head John saw a face bleak with the horrors of their voyage around Britain. Three months! What had they eaten, he wondered? What water did they have?

A man heaved a seaman's chest out of the boat and was immediately mobbed by villagers. They broke it open and pulled out linen, a hat with a feather, a silver tankard. The man began to shout and gesticulate. Those who were able to stand gathered around him, and John guessed he was an officer.

The local constable took charge. He sent someone to alert the authorities in Plymouth and began to round up the prisoners. There seemed to be a hundred or more. Men were still coming out of the sea, some half-naked, some injured and streaming blood. The villagers swooped among the strangers' possessions, their voices shrill, like gulls. Kate was caught by the excitement.

'Look! Gold ducats!' She held one up.

In the struggle a purse had spilt its contents and coins glinted among the pebbles. Kate stooped to find more.

'John, look!'

But John had noticed something happening a little way off, under the lee of the Shippen Rock, where the beach gave way to long seams of dark rock with watery channels between. A group of boys: Walt Farley, Kit Reddaway and the Jenner twins. What were they doing? There was something furtive and threatening about the way they were moving. He went to see, jumping from rock to rock.

They'd got a man cornered – a survivor from the wreck. They were jeering at him and pelting him with stones – only small stones, but John could see how they struck and hurt.

The man was crouching, his arms raised to shield his face. He was a common seaman, barefoot, wearing only breeches and a ragged shirt; his hair was long and matted, tied back with string. On a chain around his neck was a pewter medallion, and from time to time he clutched at this and called on the Virgin Mary. He was bone-thin, his eyes sunk in deep hollows.

The boys, excited by his distress, flung more stones. John saw one of them strike the man's forehead and draw blood. The others cheered.

'Papist!' yelled Kit Reddaway. He smiled at John – a smile that said, 'You're with us, aren't you?'

The man looked up and caught John's gaze. A

look of entreaty came into his eyes. '*Socorro!*' he begged. '*Socorro!*'

John remembered the dying boy from the *Maria Juan*. He, too, had called for help, but John had cursed him. He was Spanish; his people had killed John's father and maimed Luke Fewings.

Walt Farley threw another stone. 'Coward!' he shouted.

Coward. John thought of the Spanish ships with blood running from their scuppers. Whatever they were, the Dons were not cowards.

But the other boys took up the cry: 'Coward! Coward!' George Jenner picked up a larger stone and hurled it, cutting the man's cheekbone.

'No!' John shouted.

The boys turned and stared.

'They are not cowards!' said John. 'None of them! They fought like – like heroes, to the very end.' He strode forward and pushed Walt Farley aside. 'You don't know what it was like.'

'They're dogs! Papist dogs...' But the other boys fell back, startled by John's anger.

The man stared, looking from one to another of them. Still on his knees, he began to gabble in Spanish.

John remembered the sick and starving English

seamen falling exhausted in the streets of Margate – ordinary men with no choices, pressed into the Queen's service.

We are all the same, he realised. This man is not my enemy.

The man was still talking to him in Spanish. The boys had drifted away.

'Don't be afraid,' John said. 'You'll be taken prisoner, but you won't be ill-treated.'

He hoped it was true. His father had died, but perhaps this man would be luckier. Perhaps one day he'd go home.

'Come,' he said. 'I'll help you.'

And he reached out a hand.

POSTSCRIPT

The *San Pedro Mayor*, wrecked at Hope Cove in November 1588, was the last ship of the Armada to sink off the British coast. All the prisoners from this ship eventually went home to Spain.

Glossary

Aftercastle   The part of the main deck of a ship towards the stern

Bilge water   Dirty water that collects inside the bottom of a boat

Boatswain   Officer in charge of the maintenance of the ship

Breech   Back of a gun barrel

Broadside   The simultaneous firing of all the guns on one side

Capstans   A device consisting of a revolving drum used for winding cables in

Cudgel   A heavy stick used as a weapon

Culverin shot   Ammunition for a long range cannon

Don   A title used before a man's name in Spain

Fleur-de-lis   A symbol made up of three petals tied by a band

Forecastle   The raised section of deck at the bow of a ship

Gang plank   A bridge or plank used when boarding or leaving a ship

Grappling hook   A device consisting of several hooks for grasping and holding; often thrown with a rope

Gun-port   An opening in a ship through which a cannon is fired

Keel-hauled   To drag somebody on a rope from one side of the ship to the other under the keel as a form of punishment

Larboard   The left hand side of a ship

Litany   A series of sung or spoken prayers

Oakum   Fibres from old ropes unravelled and soaked in tar.

Orlop deck   Lowest deck of a ship with three or more decks

Outlier   A ship separated from the main fleet

Pikeman   A soldier armed with a pike (a long pole with a pointed metal head)

Pressed men   Men who were forced into military service

Prow   The forward part of a ship

Rearguard   A detachment assigned to protect the rear of a (retreating) military body

Shipwrights   A builder or repairer of ships

Shot   Ammunition

Starboard   The right hand side of the ship

Scabbard   A sheath, hanging from a belt, for a sword, dagger, or bayonet

Mizzen   A sail on a mizzenmast. The mizzenmast was the third mast from the back on a ship with three or more masts

Stern   The rear part of a ship

Saker   A small cannon

Spar   A pole used to support
                             rigging on a ship

Topgallant yard   A ship's mast that is taller
                             than a topmast or is an
                             extension of a topmast

Vanguard   the military divisions of a navy
                             (or army) that lead the
                             advance into battle